This igloo book belongs to:

....

igloobooks

Published in 2020
by Igloo Books Ltd
Cottage Farm
Sywell
NN6 0BJ
www.igloobooks.com

0620 003
2 4 6 8 10 9 7 5 3
ISBN 978-1-78810-408-1

Written by Stephanie Moss
Illustrated by Natasha Rimmington

Designed by Justine Ablett
Edited by Stephanie Moss

Printed and manufactured in China

THERE'S NO PLACE LIKE home

igloobooks

The farm animals were bored. They wanted something to do.
"Our life here is so dull," said Horse. "Let's all go somewhere new!"

So they packed up their belongings
and they said their last goodbyes.
Then the farmer found them gone.
He couldn't believe his eyes!

Gone for adventure!

First they built a rocket and they **WHOOSHED** up into space.

They even took a great big tasty picnic, just in case.

But none of them could quite get used to floating everywhere.

So they flew back down to Earth so they could see what else was there.

They tried exploring in the jungle, with creatures of every kind.

It was nothing like the super-boring farm they'd left behind!

Then there were snakes and creepy-crawlies. Everything from big to small.
"Ahhh, I'm scared!" cried Sheep. "This wasn't what I'd planned at all!"

"That wasn't for us," said Horse.
"I think you'll all agree."
But then he cried, "I've got it!
Why don't we learn to ski?"

So they
WHIZZED
down snowy hilltops...

... and enjoyed the mountain breeze.

It was their best adventure yet...

... till Goat got

lost in the trees.

Next they all got tickets to a theme park, just for fun.

The rides were so amazing, they could hardly pick just one.

RAINBOW ROLLER COASTER

WAIT HERE

NEXT RIDE IN
one hour

"Let's go on the roller coaster," said Hen. "Come on, it's this way!"

But it was so busy, they just stood in line all day.

One day, Cow was feeling brave. "Let's all *skydive!*" she said.

She gave each animal a parachute and goggles for their head.

So they jumped into the air after counting down from ten.

"Woo-hoo! That was fun," she said. "Can we do it again?"

Instead they had a cosy campfire. Everyone gathered around.
But as they put up their tent, they heard a big, loud, **BOOMING** sound.

A storm went **crash-bang-flash** and the rain started to pour.

"Oh, no!" they all cried. "We don't like this any more!"

So they all boarded the deck of a 5-star luxury cruise.

Some spent every day sunbathing, while others had a snooze.

Horse just loved the ocean and
one day he dived right in.

But he quickly swam away
when he saw a pointy fin.

They tried sightseeing in the city and partying all night.

But they just didn't feel at home. Not one place they'd tried felt right.

"Maybe our plan for adventure was the wrong one all along?"
Not one place they'd been had felt like somewhere they belonged.

They returned home to the farm and they shouted out, "Yippee!"
Everything that once seemed boring felt as perfect as could be.

"We had a great adventure, but we never would have guessed
that of everywhere we've been to, we think we like home the best."

There's no place like home...